I'M FLYING!

by ALAN WADE

pictures by PETRA MATHERS

Alfred A. Knopf   New York

This is a Borzoi Book published by Alfred A. Knopf, Inc.

Text copyright © 1990 by Alan Wade
Illustrations copyright © 1990 by Petra Mathers
All rights reserved under International and Pan-American Copyright
Conventions. Published in the United States by Alfred A. Knopf, Inc., New York,
and simultaneously in Canada by Random House of Canada Limited, Toronto.
Distributed by Random House, Inc., New York.

Manufactured in Singapore
Book design by Mina Greenstein   10 9 8 7 6 5 4 3 2 1

Library of Congress Cataloging-in-Publication Data
Wade, Alan. I'm flying! / by Alan Wade; illustrations by Petra Mathers.   p.   cm.
Summary: A little boy floats away on his balloon across mountains, plains,
cities, and the sea, till he lands on a desert island.
ISBN 0-394-84510-2   ISBN 0-394-94510-7 (lib. bdg.)
[1. Balloons—Fiction. 2. Balloon ascensions—Fiction] I. Mathers, Petra, ill.
II. Title. PZ7.W11378 Im 1990 [E]—dc19   88-31360

to Gage

A.W.

to Myra and Bill

P.M.

ONCE I lived with my parents, a big dog named Thunderbird, and a mean cat named Tiger in a small pink house in the middle of a lot of other small houses. I knew there had to be more to the world, but where was it?

One day my old friend from the park, Mr. Witherspoon, gave me a box. Inside were weather balloons and a tank of helium to make them float. When I filled up a balloon, it rose in the air—and almost took me with it!

An idea exploded in my head. I tied my math book to a small balloon. Then I carried it outside and watched all those problems float up and out of sight, east over the mountains, where I would never have to solve them again.

After that I sent up everything I didn't like: Mom's purple dress, my Sunday shoes, my comb and toothbrush, Tiger and Thunderbird, and even my teacher, Miss Follendorf. Never again would I have to brush my teeth! Never again would Thunderbird bite the top off my ice cream cone!

I couldn't stop. Up went a horrible pink shirt Aunt Viola
had given me, most of my father's underwear, the dining
room chairs, a hat stand, the lawn mower. Mr. Witherspoon
helped me attach dozens of balloons to my mother's piano,
and together we watched it soar into the sky like a majestic
black bird.

"Where the heck is everything disappearing to?" my father shouted. He thought it was robbers. My mother thought it was the neighbors. No one guessed balloons.

While my parents were burning hamburgers in the backyard, Mr. Witherspoon and I tried to make the family car fly. We tied on balloon after balloon, but it wouldn't budge.

Finally, with the one hundredth balloon, the car lifted gently off the ground. It didn't exactly soar, but floated just above the driveway, light as a feather. I could bounce it with one finger like a beachball! I got behind the wheel while Mr. Witherspoon attached Thunderbird's leash to the bumper and walked me around the block.

That night I dreamed that Mr. Witherspoon blew up a giant balloon and inside I could see the whole world, as in a crystal ball. Suddenly before me were Australian kangaroos, African giraffes, Arctic reindeer, mountains and oceans, cities filled with exotic people, and a beautiful tropical island, all as clear as if they were right there.

I made up my mind to go. Early the next morning, I loaded candy, soda pop, Dad's umbrella, binoculars, and a flashlight onto an old lawn chair, tied sixteen big balloons to it, and when Mr. Witherspoon let go...I was flying!

"Good-bye, my boy! Have a good trip!" called Mr. Witherspoon.

"So long!" I shouted back. Already my friend looked tiny.

It was just like being in an elevator, only it didn't stop! Up
and up and up through the clouds I went as the sun rose over
the mountains and shone on my balloons. I floated east, like
Tiger and Thunderbird and my shoes, past crows and eagles,
and airplanes whose passengers thought they were dreaming.
I ate the candy, drank the soda, and enjoyed the view. It was
the greatest adventure of my life.

I looked way down to deep green valleys where ants were riding bicycles and driving cars. Dark clouds rolled through the mountains from the north, the wind howled, and suddenly I was soaking wet! Thunder roared and rattled my head. I wasn't *under* a storm, I was *in* it. There was rain everywhere; it was like being inside a dishwasher. I needed *ten* umbrellas.

Then the sun came out, and it was so close it dried me in a minute. The wind blew me over a plain, flat and yellow with wheat and corn all the way to the horizon.

Next came a large city, with the tops of its tallest buildings beneath me. Window washers hanging from the sides of skyscrapers waved. Tourists took my picture. I bet I was in all the newspapers.

At last there was nothing but sea and sky. I was starting to feel lonely when a sea gull landed on the foot of my chair and began to clean his feathers. To make him stay, I fed him some candy and named him Carl.

Once he finished the candy, Carl began to peck at the balloons as if they were jellybeans. One by one they started to pop.

I was falling! I closed my eyes, held my breath, and waited for the splash.

But instead I felt a *thunk!* and heard a loud chord, way out of tune. When the clouds parted, I saw that I had landed on a piano that was floating lazily above the waves under a canopy of balloons. Mom's piano! Saved by the piano I'd always hated.

But my extra weight was too much for the balloons, and we started sinking toward the sea. Carl was sitting on the keyboard, watching the fish get closer.

"Mayday, Carl, Mayday!" I shouted. "Take me to dry land before I drown!"

Carl cawed and a bunch of sea gulls swooped down out of the sky. They grabbed the balloon strings and began pulling me toward a speck on the horizon.

The speck grew into a green spot, and then a tropical island, with palm trees and beautiful beaches. Carl and his friends dropped me gently on the sand.

The trees were full of fruit, the jungle full of animals, and I made a hut out of palm leaves. I decided to stay.

I wasn't homesick, since everything I had sent up with balloons had come down on the island. There was the hat stand, my toothbrush, the dining room chairs. Tiger and Thunderbird were there too, both sweet and gentle in their beautiful new home. Even Miss Follendorf was wearing a grass skirt and dancing on the beach!

Above us the piano and the sea gulls slowly circled the island like a flying symphony.

So we passed the time, and it was a long while before I remembered my house or my parents or Mr. Witherspoon. But then a balloon arrived with a sign that said, "Come home, son!" and suddenly I thought, uh oh, I bet I'm late for dinner.